A B C D

E F G H

I J K L

M N O P

P Q R S

T U V W

X Y Z *

親子共學英語從這本繪本開始吧！

　　看到這本繪本時，第一個映入眼簾的是生動又吸睛的插畫，而且非常貼心的附上英語朗讀QR Code，家長就不用太擔心自己英語發音不準確，或是自己英語能力不夠好，無法勝任陪伴孩子透過繪本學英語這件事嘍！

　　書中依不同主題呈現日常實用詞彙與生活對話，讓大小讀者感受到這些字彙與句子都是能立即在生活當中應用。學習語言，要用得到，才會記得住，而這本繪本的內容扣緊了真實生活情境，學了之後可以隨時隨地在實際生活中練習與活用。

　　此外，閱讀時不一定要按照頁次順序來帶領孩子共讀共學，可以對應目前的生活情境與時令來找書中相關主題進行閱讀與學習。比如現在是冬天，就可以帶孩子看「冬天」這個主題單元；或是要帶孩子到商店採買物品之前，也可以先帶孩子閱讀「去購物」這個單元。

　　學習不能與生活脫鉤，一旦學習與生活有緊密的聯繫，一方面可以增強孩子的學習興趣與動機，一方面孩子學了可以在生活中實際應用，這樣學習才是孩子所需要的，否則等孩子進入國小、國中，英語對他們來說變成是一門要考試的學科，孩子永遠感受不到英語作為一種溝通工具的重要與必須性。

　　誠摯推薦這本繪本給有心啟動與孩子共學英語之路的爸爸媽媽們。

　　　　　　——李貞慧（水瓶面面）
　　　　　　國中英語教師暨閱讀推廣人

contents ｜ 目 次

孩子的第一本
情境學習英語繪本

Greetings

問候

Hi!
嗨！

Hello.
哈囉！你好！

What's up?
你好嗎？

Nice to meet you!
很高興認識你！

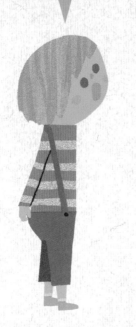

A Day
一天

Good morning.
早安。

Rise and shine.
起床嘍！

I'm still sleepy.
我還想睡。

Where are you going?
你要去哪裡？

To the library.
去圖書館。

I have to go now.
我該走了。

Catch you later.
稍後見。

A Week

一星期

Are you ready?
準備好了嗎？

I'm ready.
準備好了。

Monday
星期一

Let's share this.
我們一起分享。

Sounds great.
聽起來不錯。

Tuesday
星期二

Have a nice weekend!
周末愉快！

Thanks. You, too.
謝謝。你也是。

Friday
星期五

What's his name?
牠叫什麼名字？

How cute!
好可愛啊！

Nice to meet you.
很高興認識你。

Saturday
星期六

I don't have a clue.
我完全沒有頭緒。

have no idea.
我不知道。

Wednesday
星期三

I'm moved.
我好感動。

Same here.
我也是。

Thursday
星期四

Oh my!
噢，天啊！

Sorry.
對不起。

Oops.
糟了。

Better luck next time!
下次再接再厲！

Don't worry.
沒關係。

Sunday
星期日

In the Garden

花園裡

In the Bathroom
浴室裡

towel
浴巾

Just a minute.
再等一下。

Quick, quick!
快一點，快一點！

OCCUPIED
使用中

Go ahead.
你先請。

knock knock
叩！叩！

cup
漱口杯

faucet
水龍頭

toothbrush
牙刷

brush brush
刷——刷——

I've overslept.
我睡過頭了。

Are your hands clean?
你的手乾淨嗎？

kitten
小貓

cat
貓

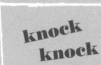
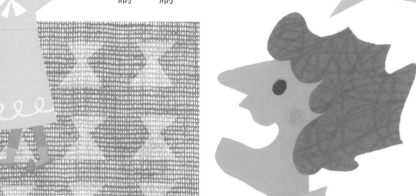

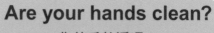

At the Front Door

在前門

roof
屋頂

house
房子

Have a good day.
祝你有美好的一天。

I'm all set.
我都準備好了。

You forgot this.
你忘了這個。

Take care.
小心喔！

Bye.
再見。

See you later.
晚點見。

In the Kitchen

廚房裡

Yummy cake ♪
美味的蛋糕 ♪

It looks delicious.
看起來很好吃。

Break the eggs.
把蛋殼敲開。

Mix the eggs
把蛋汁攪勻。

cut
切

peel
削皮

slice
切片

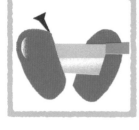

chop
剁碎

fry
煎

frying pan
煎鍋

It smells good.
好香啊！

oven
烤箱

Oh my!
噢，天啊！

I'm sorry.
抱歉。

It's OK.
沒關係。

Make balls.
揉成麵團。

grill
燒烤

bake
烘焙

deep-fry
炸

boil
煮

stew
燉

In the Living Room

Looks like you're having fun.
看來你很愉快。

What's on TV now?
現在電視上在播什麼？

potted plant
盆栽

Come on!
來啊！
開始吧！

Way to go!
做得好！

Peek-a-boo!
躲貓貓！

chair
椅子

cradle
搖籃

Goo-goo.
咕——
咕——

In the Bedroom

臥室裡

What's your dream?
你的夢想是什麼？

Time to go to bed.
該睡覺嘍！

Hmm...
嗯……

...let me see.
讓我想想看。

I'm not sleepy.
我還不想睡。

I want to be an astronaut.
我想當太空人。

spaceship
太空船

starry sky
星空

the moon
月亮

light
燈

What a lot of stars!
好多星星啊！

globe
地球儀

telescope
天文望遠鏡

How beautiful!
好美麗啊！

Let me take a look.
讓我看一下。

model
模型

picture book
圖畫書

Birthday Party

生日派對

Thank you.
謝謝。

Happy Birthday!
生日快樂！

You're stepping on my dress.
你踩到我的洋裝了。

Oops! Sorry.
噢，抱歉。

You're gorgeous!
你真漂亮！

You look good in it.
你穿這件衣服很好看。

Let me through.
借過。

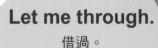

How many candles do we need?
我們需要幾支蠟燭？

I caught you.
我抓到你了。

cake
蛋糕

candle
蠟燭

Yummy!
好吃！

Don't tell anybody.
不要告訴別人。

Maybe...
也許……

dish
盤子

Just between you and me.
這是你和我之間的祕密。

It looks yummy.
看起來很好吃。

So sweet.
好甜啊！

Time to Play

遊戲時間

Great!
太好了！

Fantastic!
太厲害了！

hula-hoop
呼啦圈

Excellent!
非常好！

Let me play, too.
請讓我一起玩。

Whose turn?
該誰了？

My turn.
該我了。

Hee-hee-hee.
嘻嘻嘻。

Hang on.
等一下！

Hmm.
哼嗯。

Around Town

城鎮上

church
教堂

Don't worry.
別擔心。

I'm scared.
我害怕。

What's the matter?
怎麼回事？

priest
神父

No problem.
沒問題。

Oh boy
噢，天啊

Excuse me.
不好意思。

Go straight and turn left.
直走，然後左轉。

fountain
噴泉

bride
新娘

Where's the church?
請問教堂在哪裡？

groom
新郎

bench
長椅

Going Shopping

去購物

Are you hungry?
你餓了嗎？

Sort of.
有點餓。

BURGER&BURGER
漢堡店

May I help you?
您需要什麼服務？

I'd like three hamburgers.
我要三個漢堡。

For here or to go?
內用，還是外帶？

To go, please.
外帶，謝謝。

tableware shop
餐具店

clothing shop
服裝店

hat shop
帽子店

Too expensive.
太貴了。

Can I try it on?
我可以試穿嗎？

Suits me?
適合我嗎？

Too big.
太大了。

Sure.
當然可以。

It's very you!
很適合你喲！

I'll take this.
我要買這個。

Can I have one?
我可以拿一個嗎？

florist
鮮花
小販

Here you are.
這個給您。

PLEASE TAKE ONE
請拿一個

At the Amusemen
在遊樂園

Yippee!
喲呵——

I'm excited!
我好興奮！

I'm thrilled!
我好激動！

ROLLER COASTER
雲霄飛車

No, let's not.
不，我們不要搭吧！

I feel dizzy.
我覺得頭暈。

Me, too
我也是。

Let's ride
the roller coaster.
我們去搭雲霄飛車吧！

It's scary.
好可怕喔！

Two kids, please.
請給我兩張兒童票。

Don't cut in.
不要插隊。

TICKETS
售票亭

On the Farm

農場上

sheep
綿羊

baa baa
咩──咩──

What does a sheep say?

綿羊怎麼叫呢？

moo moo
哞──哞──

Do you lik
animals'

你喜歡動物嗎

cow
乳牛

quack quack
呱──呱──

meow meow
喵──喵──

duck
鴨子

cat
貓

What do animals say in English?
動物怎麼叫呢？

In the Forest

森林裡

owl
貓頭鷹

Look up.
你看上面。

What's that?
那是什麼？

A dinosaur egg.
一顆恐龍蛋。

No kiddin
不可能吧！

Shh!
噓——

backpack
背包

Stay still.
不要動喔！

Let's go.
我們走吧！

All right.
好的。

stump
樹墩

How's the weather?

今天天氣如何？

It's sunny.
今天是晴天。

It's cloudy.
今天多雲。

It's windy.
今天風很大。

It's snowy.
今天下雪。

It's stormy.
今天暴風雨。

thunder
打雷

lightning
閃電

tornado
龍捲風

rainbow
彩虹

Spring

春天

cherry tree
櫻花樹

Enjoy your lunch.
好好享用你的午餐。

I could eat a horse.
我餓得可以吃下一匹馬。

Yummy!
好好吃！

horse
馬

It's comfortable.
好舒服。

It's warm.
好溫暖。

tortoise
烏龜

fish
魚

stream
溪流

Summer

夏天

6月	7月	8月
June	July	August
六月	七月	八月

May I use your bucket?
我可以用你的水桶嗎？

Sure.
當然可以。

shell
貝殼

sand castle
沙堡

beach
沙灘

play Beach Flags
搶沙灘旗遊戲

Run, run, run
跑，跑，跑！

It's so hot.
好熱啊！

It sure is.
的確很熱。

beach umbrella
海灘遮陽傘

Autumn (Fall)

秋天

Happy Halloween

萬聖節快樂

Trick or treat.
不給糖，就搗蛋。

So beautiful!
好美喔！

black cat
黑貓

Jack-o'-lantern
南瓜燈

Red, yellow, and orange leaves.
紅色、黃色和橘色的葉子。

fallen leaves
落葉

mushroom
蘑菇

What a lot of food!
好多食物喔！

squirrel
松鼠

acorn
橡實

chestnut
栗子

9月 **10月** **11月**

September **October** **November**
九月 十月 十一月

Lovely picture.
好美的景色。

It's getting cool.
天氣變得涼爽了。

Let's save them.
我們把橡實儲藏起來。

Let's eat them.
我們把橡實吃掉。

No, let's save them.
不，我們要儲藏起來。

grapes
葡萄

Winter

冬天

12月	1月	2月
December	**January**	**February**
十二月	一月	二月

snow crystal
雪花

It's freezing.
天寒地凍的。

You're right.
的確是啊！

scarf
圍巾

mittens
手套

boots
靴子

snowman
雪人

Look!
你看！

There's Santa Claus!
聖誕老人在那裡！

Ho, ho, ho!
嗬，嗬，嗬！

Merry Christmas!
聖誕快樂！

Here I come!
我來嘍！

sled
雪橇

Ahhh!
哇啊！

Get out of my way!
快讓開啊！

Duck!
快躲！

Yay!
吔！

Brrr!
抖抖抖！
（好冷喔！）

snowball fight
雪球仗

hare
野兔

Ouch!
哎喲！

Feelings

感受

How are you feeling?
你感覺如何？

happy
快樂

I feel great!
感覺很好！

worried
擔心

I'm scared.
我很害怕。

excited

興奮

satisfied

滿意

I'm fine!
我很好！

proud

得意

confident

有信心

surprised

驚訝

relieved

鬆了一口氣

disappointed

失望

angry

生氣

embarrassed

尷尬

sad

難過

Cheer up!
振奮起來！

Exercise

運動

jump

跳

squat on my heels

蹲

turn my neck around

旋轉頸部

I can shake my hips.

我可以抖動臀部。

stretch

伸展

Good job!

做得好！

lie down

平躺

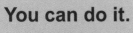

You can do it.
你辦得到。

run
跑

walk
走

Yes! I can lift!
是的！我舉得起來！

I'm exhausted.
我好累。

take a deep breath
深呼吸

Don't give up.
不要放棄。

bend my knees
屈膝

clap my hands
拍掌

Health
健康

I have a runny nose.
我流鼻水了。

I can't stop coughing.
我咳嗽個不停。

I have a fever.
我發燒了。

I have a cold.
我感冒了。

I have hay fever.
我得了過敏性花粉症。

Put on your mask.
戴上口罩。

What's the matter?
你怎麼了？

Ouch!
哎喲！

A, atchooooo!
哈——啾——

I have a sore throat.
我喉嚨痛。

I have a toothache.
我牙齒痛。

I have a headache.
我頭痛。

Are you OK?
你沒事吧？

I have a stomachache.
我胃痛。

You look pale.
你臉色蒼白。

Bless you!
祝你平安健康！

I feel sick.
我不舒服。

Take this medicine.
把藥吃了。

監修／外山節子

日本敬和學園大學前客座教授。新潟小學英語教育研究會顧問。主要的著作有「英語時間」系列、《兒童英語指導手冊》（以上暫譯）等，監修著作亦豐富。

繪圖／手塚明美

生長於日本橫濱。曾任職視覺設計公司，於 1998 年起擔任自由接案插畫家。作品包括與語言學習相關的書籍、雜誌插畫，也販售廣告、雜誌、文具等相關雜貨。興趣是帶狗散步。現居東京。

翻譯／林劭貞

兒童文學工作者，從事翻譯與教學研究。喜歡文字，貪戀圖像，人生目標是玩遍各種形式的圖文創作。翻譯作品有《「不要、不行、我不去！」大聲嚇阻陌生人，建立孩童自我保護的能力》、《令人怦然心動的看漫畫學英文片語300：從浪漫愛情故事，激發學習熱情，提升英語理解力！》、《小朋友的廚房：一起動手做家庭料理》等；插畫作品有《魔法二分之一》、《魔法湖畔》和《天鵝的翅膀：楊喚的寫作故事》（以上皆由小熊出版）。

英語學習

孩子的第一本情境學習英語繪本：The Picture Book of English Phrases That Make You Happy
監修：外山節子 | 繪圖：手塚明美 | 翻譯：林劭貞

協力編輯・音檔製作：高津由紀子
英語校對：愛德華・華因茲洛（Edward Winslow）
英語旁白：戶田達里奧、茱莉亞・亞瑪柯夫（Julia Yermakov）
企畫・設計：村田弘子

總編輯：鄭如瑤 | 主編：陳玉娥 | 編輯：張雅惠 | 美術編輯：張雅玫
行銷副理：塗幸儀 | 行銷企畫：林怡伶、許博雅 | 錄音：許伯琴・印笛錄音製作有限公司

出版：小熊出版／遠足文化事業股份有限公司
發行：遠足文化事業股份有限公司（讀書共和國出版集團）
地址：231新北市新店區民權路108-3號6樓 | 電話：02-22181417 | 傳真：02-86672166
劃撥帳號：19504465 | 戶名：遠足文化事業股份有限公司
Facebook：小熊出版 | E-mail：littlebear@bookrep.com.tw

讀書共和國出版集團網路書店：www.bookrep.com.tw
客服專線：0800-221029 | 客服信箱：service@bookrep.com.tw
團體訂購請洽業務部：02-22181417 分機1124
法律顧問：華洋法律事務所／蘇文生律師 | 印製：凱林彩印股份有限公司
初版一刷：2019年1月 | 二版一刷：2024年2月 | 定價：350元
ISBN：978-626-7429-07-5 | 書號：0BEL4011

Original Japanese title: Hajimete no Eigo de Oshaberi Ehon
Originally published in Japanese by PIE International in 2010
PIE International Inc.
2-32-4, Minami-Otsuka, Toshima-ku, Tokyo 170-0005 JAPAN
Copyright © 2010 akemi tezuka / hiroko murata / PIE International
All rights reserved. No part of this publication may be reproduced in any form or by any means, graphic, electronic or mechanical, including photocopying and recording by an information storage and retrieval system, without permission in writing from the publisher.

小熊出版讀者回函

小熊出版官方網頁

國家圖書館出版品預行編目（CIP）資料

孩子的第一本情境學習英語繪本：The picture book of English phrases that make you happy / 外山節子監修；手塚明美繪圖；林劭貞翻譯. -- 二版. -- 新北市：小熊出版，遠足文化事業股份有限公司，2024.02
48面；21.4x28.4 公分. --（英語學習）
ISBN 978-626-7429-07-5（精裝）

1.CST：英語 2.CST：讀本 3.CST：繪本

805.18   112021889

A B C D
E F G H
I J K L
* M N O
P Q R S
T U V W
X Y Z *